# Disney · PIXAR
# FINDING NEMO

Nemo shouts, "First day of school!" Nemo is excited, but his father Marlin is worried. Nemo, who has a small fin, swims awkwardly. Marlin wishes that Nemo would stay safe in their anemone.

At school, Nemo meets his teacher, Mr. Ray, and some new friends. The students climb on Mr. Ray's back to go exploring.

Marlin learns that Nemo's class went to the Drop-off, where the water is deep and dangerous. He immediately rushes after them.

At the Drop-off, Nemo's friends dare each other to swim up to a boat. Nemo does not want to. But when Marlin arrives and scolds Nemo, Nemo gets angry. He swims out to the boat. A diver captures him!

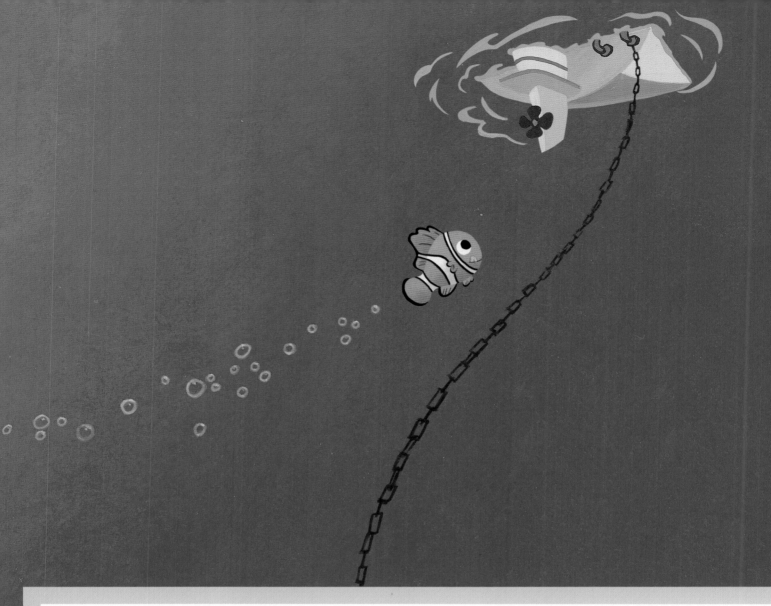

Gear Up!

Marlin chases the boat, but it speeds away.  "Has anybody seen a boat?" he yells. A fish named Dory has! She promises to lead Marlin to it.

But Dory, who forgets everything, soon forgets their search.  Even worse, a shark named Bruce swims up.  Bruce invites Marlin and Dory to a submarine for a party — of sharks!

Luckily, these sharks are on a no-fish diet. At their party, Marlin spots a mask from the diver who took Nemo. The writing on the mask might help Marlin find his son!

Then Bruce gets hungry. Marlin and Dory quickly leave! As they flee, they find a way to send a torpedo into Bruce's mouth. He spits it out into a sea mine!

# Sharks!

Far away, Nemo wakes up in a fish tank. The diver, a dentist named Dr. Sherman, took Nemo to his office. The other tank fish welcome Nemo. So does Nigel, a friendly pelican.

Nigel is shooed away by Dr. Sherman, who accidentally knocks over a picture of his niece, Darla, whose birthday is days away. "You're her present," he tells Nemo.

The other fish are horrified. Darla shakes fish!

That night, Nemo swims through the "Ring of Fire" to join the Tank Gang's club.  Gill, the tank's leader, came from the ocean like Nemo. He has a plan to get back! If Nemo can wedge a pebble in the tank's filter, the tank will get dirty. The dentist will put the fish in bags while he cleans the tank. Then they can roll their bags out the window and into the harbor.

Australia

Indian Ocean

Pacific Ocean

Southern Ocean

In the ocean, Dory remembers she can read! She reads the words on the mask:

"P. Sherman, 42 Wallaby Way, Sydney."

Some moonfish point the way to Sydney. They warn Dory that when she and Marlin come to a trench, they must swim through it, not over it.

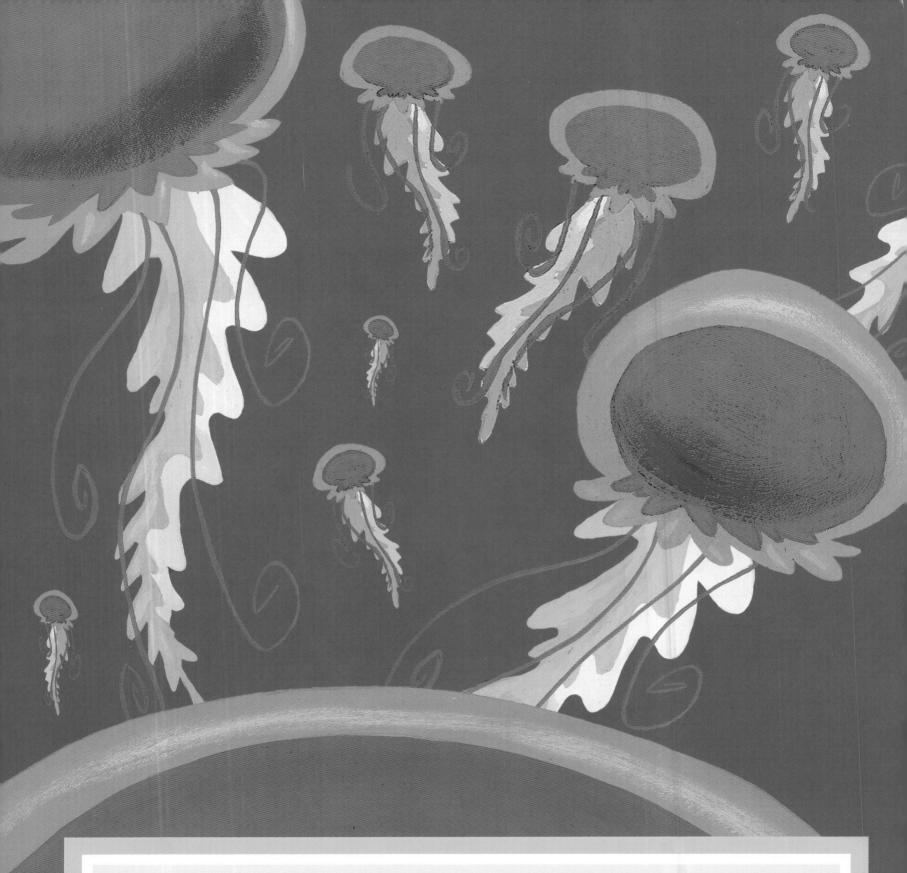

The trench looks very scary. Marlin decides to ignore Dory's warning and swim
over it. But soon he and Dory are surrounded by jellyfish!

Marlin and Dory bounce off the tops of the jellyfish, but Dory is stung.

Marlin gets them both away from the jellyfish just as he is stung and passes out.

In the tank, Nemo agrees to help with Gill's escape plan. Nemo swims right into the filter with a pebble! But the pebble pops out.  Then Nemo is almost caught by the filter's moving blades! Gill decides his plan is too risky.

Marlin wakes up when he hears someone say, "Dude! Focus, dude!" The voice belongs to a sea turtle named Crush! 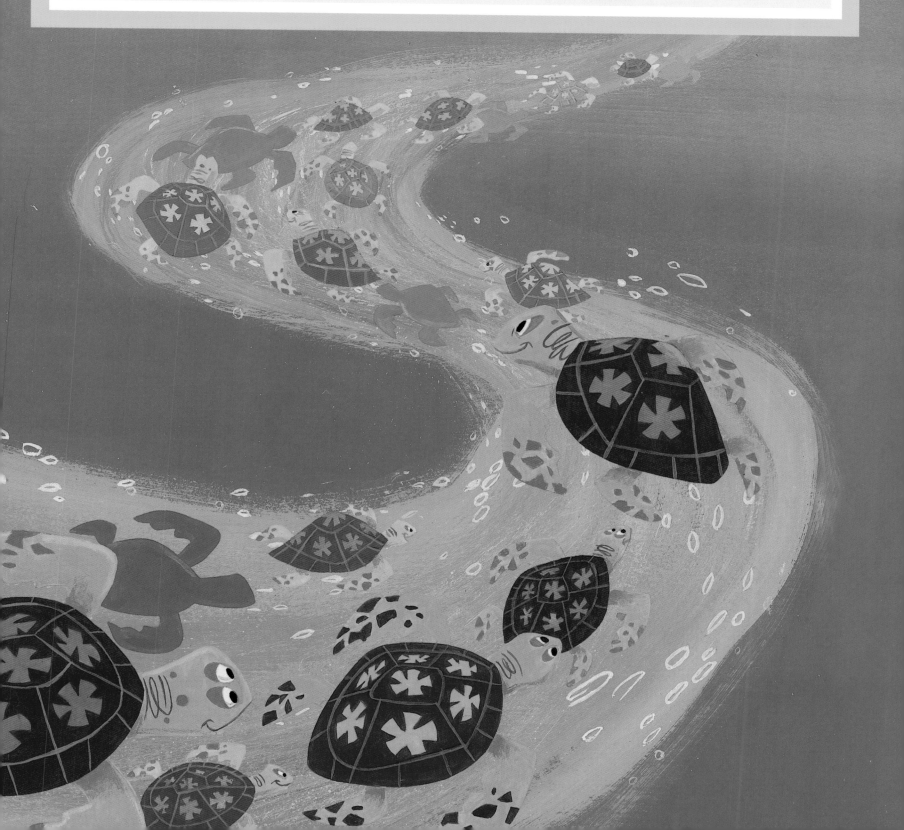 The turtles found Marlin and Dory. Now they're all riding the East Australian Current, which goes right near Sydney.

Crush's son, Squirt, asks Marlin about his journey. Marlin tells the turtles about his search for Nemo. Soon the story spreads throughout the ocean!

Near Sydney, Marlin and Dory leave the turtles. Dory asks a whale for directions.
But the whale accidentally swallows Dory and Marlin!

Luckily, Dory speaks whale. She tells Marlin that the whale says to move to the back of its throat. Marlin is scared, but he trusts Dory and does it.

The whale shoots them out of its blowhole, right into Sydney Harbor!

# Whale Tales!

Nigel carries Marlin's story to Nemo! Nemo wants to be courageous like Marlin. He tries Gill's plan again! 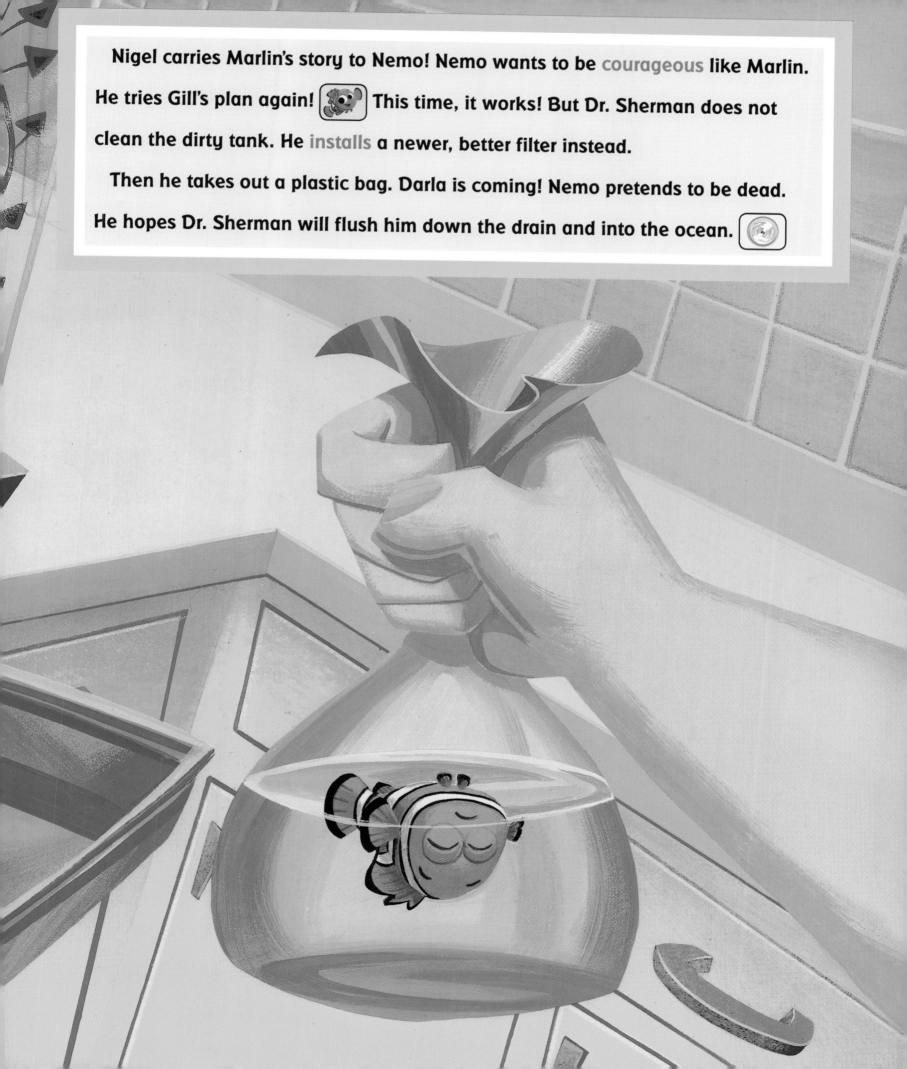 This time, it works! But Dr. Sherman does not clean the dirty tank. He installs a newer, better filter instead.

Then he takes out a plastic bag. Darla is coming! Nemo pretends to be dead. He hopes Dr. Sherman will flush him down the drain and into the ocean.

Nigel finds Marlin and Dory and flies them to the dentist's office.

Marlin sees Nemo and does not realize that Nemo is only pretending to be dead. The dentist shoos Nigel away before Marlin learns the truth.

Gill jumps out of the tank, right onto Darla's head! She drops the bag, which breaks. Gill lands on a dentist's tool and flips Nemo down the drain.

Nemo has escaped!

The drain leads to the ocean, where Nemo encounters Dory. Together, they find Marlin. Just then, Dory and some groupers are caught in a net!

Nemo has an idea about how to help them. He and Marlin tell the fish to swim downward to break the net.

Nemo, Marlin, and Dory go home and tell everyone about their adventures!